Murder within Murder

A MR. AND MRS. NORTH MYSTERY

Murder within Murder

by **Frances & Richard Lockridge**

THORNDIKE PRESS • THORNDIKE, MAINE

Library of Congress Cataloging in Publication Data:

Lockridge, Frances Louise Davis.
  Murder within murder.

  Reprint. Orginally published: Philadelphia:
J.B. Lippincott, 1946.
    1. Large type books.   I. Lockridge, Richard, 1898- .
II. Title.
[PS3523.0243M8 1985]   813'.54   84-23929
ISBN 0-89621-587-3

Large Print edition available through arrangement with Harper &
Row Publishers, New York.

Cover design by Andy Winther

Murder
within Murder

I

Miss Amelia Gipson presented a firm front to the world; she stood for no nonsense. For the conscious period of her fifty-two years she had stood for no nonsense in a world which was stubbornly nonsensical. The nonsense in the world had not been greatly abated by her attitude, but Miss Gipson's skirts were clean. What one person could do, she had done. If that was inadequate, the fault lay elsewhere; there was a laxity in higher places. Miss Gipson often suspected that there was.

She wore a gray rayon dress on this, the last evening of her life. It was fitted smoothly on her substantial body, which, although Miss Gipson was not notably a large woman, was apt to give frailer persons an impression of massiveness. It followed her firm bosom — a meticulously undivided expanse — with discretion; it

7

was snug over her corseted hips. There was a touch of white at the throat; there was a little watch hanging from a silver pin on the left side of the central expanse. Above the touch of white at the throat, Miss Gipson's face was firm and untroubled; it was a face on which assurance rode, sure of a welcome. Miss Gipson did not know that it was the last evening of her life. Nothing was further from her thoughts.

The colored elevator man in the Holborn Annex greeted her with docile respect and rather as if he expected her to smell his breath. She had complained to the management on one occasion that there had been, in George's car, an unmistakable odor of liquor. She had indicated a belief that it might have had its origin in George. She had pointed out that an elevator operated by a person under the influence of alcohol was a menace to the tenants. The management had listened, nodding agreement, and had taken it up.

"Beer ain't liquor," George had insisted. "I had me a beer. A beer ain't liquor."

Anything was liquor to Miss Gipson, the management thought, fleetingly, and as it thought of Miss Gipson had a sudden, unaccountable longing for a drink. But the management merely cautioned George, a little vaguely, not to let it happen again. He hoped, this

8

evening, that Miss Gipson would not detect that it had happened again.

Miss Gipson was not thinking of George. She had collected her mail at the desk when she came in, and the top letter was addressed to Miss Amelia Gibson. Miss Gipson's eyes had hardened when she saw this, and realized that the world was at its nonsense again. There was no reason why the world, including department stores with fur collections to announce, should not learn that Miss Gipson's name was spelled with a *p*, instead of a common *b*. Miss Gipson had had a good deal of trouble with the world about this and resignedly expected to have more. It was not that she did not make the difference clear.

"Gip-son," she had always said, with the clearest possible enunciation. "With a *P*, not a *B*. Gi*p*-son."

But the world was slovenly. To the world, Gipson sounded very like Gibson, and Gibson was easier. So Miss Gipson was, except by those who knew her best, almost always incorrectly addressed, and this did nothing to lessen her conviction that things were, in general, very badly run. They had been badly run as long as she could remember, and her memory started, with clarity, at the age of five. Of late years, things had been worse run than before, if anything.

"Good evening," Miss Gipson said to George, automatically and without sniffing. She said nothing more and George said nothing more until the car stopped at the tenth floor of the Holburn Annex. Miss Gipson stepped firmly out and went firmly down the corridor — down the middle of the corridor — to her door. She opened it and went in to her one-room furnished apartment, with bath, and laid her letters on the coffee table — from which Miss Gipson never drank coffee — which was in front of the sofa, on which Miss Gipson never lounged. She took off her hat and put it on the closet shelf and went to the bathroom and washed her face in lukewarm water. She dried her face and did not examine it further, knowing what it looked like. She washed her hands. She went back and sat down, erectly, on the sofa and opened her letters, beginning with the first one. She looked at it, sniffed — Miss Gipson did not wear furs, and disapproved of those who did — put it back in its envelope and laid it on the coffee table. She laid it so that it squared with the oblong of the table. She picked up the next letter.

It was correctly addressed. It began: "Dear Aunt Amelia." The writing of the letter was almost like printing; to it there was a certain flagrance, a kind of impertinence. But the content of the letter was straight-forward, almost blunt. Miss Gipson read it and sat for a moment looking at it.

"Well!" Miss Gipson said to herself. "She will, will she? Nonsense!"

Miss Gipson read the letter again, and smiled a little. She looked at the postmark and smiled again. By this time Nora would have got her letter; by this time Nora would know better, as she should have known from the beginning. That nonsense was going to end; that nonsense had, in fact, ended. No niece of hers. . . . Miss Gipson let the thought go unfinished. She took up the next letter. It, also, was correctly addressed. It began: "Dear Amelia." Miss Gipson read it and her eyes narrowed. She read it again and put it down on her lap and looked at the opposite wall without seeing it clearly. It was as if she were looking through the opposite wall out into a world full of nonsense — reprehensible nonsense. Miss Gipson's face was not expressive, and there was no one there to attempt its reading. But it was for a moment troubled; for a moment confidence was uneasy on it. There was more than one kind of nonsense in the world, Miss Gipson thought.

"But," she reminded herself, "there are more ways than one of killing a cat, too."

She put the letter down on top of the one which began "Dear Aunt Amelia" and opened her fourth letter. She merely glanced at it and put it down on the letter advertising furs. She made it expressly clear that she had no intention of paying good money for unsatisfactory merchandise, war or no war. If storekeepers chose to disregard her irrefutable statements, the responsibility – and the inevitable chagrin – were theirs. Miss Gipson's position had been stated.

She sat for a moment and then picked up the letter which began "Dear Amelia" and read it again. She also read again the letter from Nora. Then she put these two letters in a pigeonhole of a small secretary. She put the other two letters in a wastebasket, after tearing them twice across. She thought a moment, took out the letter which had contained a bill she had no intention of paying, and tore it into even small fragments. It was entirely possible that the maid who cleaned the room read letters thrown into the wastebasket, piecing them together like crossword puzzles. There was, certainly, little to indicate that she did much else in the room. Miss Gipson absently ran a finger along the writing shelf of the secretary and looked at it. She made a small, disparaging sound with her tongue and teeth. Nonsense! War or no war, an apartment hotel like the Annex could manage to get proper help. The management was shiftless and indifferent. It permitted chambermaids not only to neglect their jobs, but to wear perfume while doing it. Miss Gipson sniffed. More than usual, this time, and a new brand. No improvement, however; there were no gradations in perfume, so far as Miss Gipson could tell. All represented laxity, at the best. At the worst they were invitations to the most nonsensical of human activities. It was an activity in which Miss Gipson had never had a part, and which — she hardly needed to assure herself — she had no interest. Wherein, it had to be admitted, she differed from far too much of the world. Miss Gipson had no illusion that the particular nonsense to which perfume — and much else you could see and hear and in other fashions not ignore — invited, was of limited scope. Miss Gipson saw it, in its secondary manifestations, to be sure, everywhere. She had disapproved of it since she was ten; her disapproval had never faltered.

"Chambermaids!" Miss Gipson thought. "Boys, nothing but boys. And Nora."

Miss Gipson would not have spoken thus scatteredly. Her conversation was never scattered. But her thoughts, as she so often had occasion to point out, were her own.

13

She looked at the watch. It told her the time was ten minutes of six. Then the telephone rang.

"Miss Gipson speaking," she said, as soon as she picked up the telephone. She waited a moment for the inevitable readjustment to take place. "*This* is Miss Gipson," she said. She said it in the tone of forbearance she had used so often when she had a desk of her own at the college, before it became necessary for her to resign because nonsense — and worse than nonsense — was so widespread even at Ward; before it was clear that, even there, the moral laxity which was demoralizing the world was creeping in. Not that the world's morality, even at its best, had ever met Miss Gipson's standards.

"Yes, John?" Miss Gipson said into the telephone. Her tone was not inviting. She listened.

"There is no reason for any further discussion," she said. "And in any case, I am occupied this evening."

She listened again.

"There is no use going over that again, John," she said. "I am perfectly aware that it says at my discretion. I am exercising my discretion. Mr. Backley entirely agrees."

She listened again, briefly.

"I can only advise patience, John," she said.

"It is an excellent virtue. I am sure my dear brother meant you to learn patience when he made his very wise arrangements about you and your sister."

She listened again.

"About that, also, I must exercise my discretion," she said. "You can tell your sister so. I have already told her. She cannot expect me to be a party to what I consider immorality."

The answer was apparently only a word or two — perhaps only a word.

"Immorality," Amelia Gipson repeated, without emotion. "I call it what it is. Nora cannot expect me to countenance any such action. I shall certainly make the situation clear to the person concerned if she makes it necessary. I've told her that."

She listened again, for the last time.

"I do not care if I am the only person in the world who takes what you call that attitude," she said. "So much the worse for the world. Right is right, John. Goodbye."

She hung up. She nodded her head slightly, approving herself. She looked at her watch. It was six o'clock. She shook her head in slight annoyance over that. She got her hat from the closet and put it on without consulting a mirror. She checked the contents of her orderly handbag. She looked around the orderly room

15

and left it, locking the door behind her. She had insisted on a special lock, which she could make sure of with her own key.

George was no longer on the elevator. There was a girl operating it and there was a faint scent of perfume in the car; it was not, Miss Gipson thought, the same scent she had noticed in her apartment. Otherwise she would have thought that this was the chambermaid on her floor. The girl said "good evening" and Miss Gipson slightly inclined her head without replying. She would not encourage the nonsense of girls as elevator operators.

The doorman also said "good evening" to Miss Gipson. She replied to him, in a clear, decisive voice which did not invite further conversation. She walked up the street to the square and the doorman looked after her and, as she turned the corner, raised his shoulders just perceptibly and for his own amusement. Quite an old girl, the doorman thought. Glad he wasn't married to her. Then he realized that was an odd thought to have in relation to Miss Gipson, although it had no doubt been widely held.

It was ten after six when Miss Gipson sat down to dinner in a tearoom near Washington Square. It was called the Green House and the door was painted green and there were ferns in the window. The waitress put the usual peg under one of the legs of Miss Gipson's table to steady it and said they had a few lamb chops and it was lucky Miss Gipson had not been a few minutes later. Miss Gipson had a lamb chop, very well done, and creamed potatoes, string beans and a salad of two slices of tomato and a lettuce leaf with a rather sour dressing. She had a piece of cocoanut cake and a cup of tea, and caught an uptown Fifth Avenue bus at a few minutes before seven.

It was twenty minutes past seven when Miss Gipson entered the New York Public Library for the last time. Since she had been working regularly at the Library for several weeks and had worked close to schedule during afternoons and evenings, it was subsequently possible to trace her movements with fair exactitude. She had entered one of the elevators at around seven-thirty or a little before, and had got off at the third floor. She had turned in slips for "Famous American Murders," by Algernon Bentley; "The Trial of Martha West," one of the Famous Trials series; and for magazine articles on the unsolved murder of Lorraine Purdy—unsolved largely because of the disappearance of Frank Purdy, whom Lorraine had unwisely married — and the presumably solved domestic crime wave which had taken off the elderly Mrs. William Rogers and her daughter, Susan, together with a maid who had unwisely eaten what remained of some chicken à la king which had been prepared primarily for Mrs. Rogers but had been, in the end, rather too widely distributed. Mrs. Rogers' nephew had been suspected of adding an unorthodox ingredient to the chicken à la king, but there had been other possibilities. The nephew, whose name was Samuel King, had been somewhat halfheartedly convicted by a jury, which resolved its doubts by bringing in a second-degree verdict, to the freely expressed annoyance of Justice Ryerson.

Amelia Gipson had received the books and the bound volumes of the magazines in which the articles appeared in the North Reading Room. At about nine o'clock, or a few minutes later, she had been seen by one of the attendants leaving the catalogue room through the main door. A few minutes later she had returned. She had been absent about long enough to walk to a drinking fountain down the corridor, the attendant thought.

At a quarter of ten, fifteen minutes before the library closed, Miss Gipson became violently ill at her seat at one of the long tables. She died in the emergency ward of Bellevue Hospital at about eleven o'clock. Sodium fluoride poisoning had been diagnosed promptly; but Miss Gipson had not responded to treatment.

18

II

Mr. North was reading a manuscript and the word *No* was slowly forming itself in his mind when the whirring started. At first it was not clearly identifiable as a whirring. It was more a kind of buzzing. It might, Jerry North thought, even be in his head. Exhaustion, possibly. Or the manuscript. He shook his head, thinking the sound might go away, and dug back into the manuscript. "It must be admitted," the manuscript said, "that in the post-war world we face an increasing agglomeration of —" Clearly, Jerry North decided, it was the manuscript. The post-war world was buzzing at him. Its shining machinery, made to a large degree out of plastic, was whirring at unimagined tasks, turning out things made largely of glass. Whatever the post-war world might finally be, it would inevitably also be a buzzing in the ears.

He put down the manuscript and covered his eyes with a hand and waited for this audible omen of the future to go away. It did not go away. It came into the living room and sat down on the sofa. If it was in his head, there was something drastically wrong with his head. A little fearfully, Mr. North parted his fingers and looked at the sofa, on which the future sat, buzzing. The future was Mrs. North, wearing an apron over a very short play suit. The future, Jerry North decided, was brighter than he had allowed himself to hope. The future was Pamela North in a checked apron over a brief play suit, with a bowl in its lap and an egg beater in its hands.

Jerry smiled at his wife, who stared into the bowl with fixed interest. A cake, Jerry decided, vaguely. It was an odd time to be making a cake. Ten o'clock — no, five after ten — in the evening was an odd time to make a cake. But when Pam made cakes — and when she made pies, as she sometimes did, and once doughnuts — it was apt to be at odd times. She had made doughnuts at an odd time, the only time she had made doughnuts. They had been to the theater and, waiting for a cab, had stepped for shelter under the awning of a store in which they were making doughnuts and serving them to people, apparently to advertise a brand of coffee. Pam had said nothing then, but when she had got home she had said suddenly that what she was hungry for was doughnuts, and why not make some? They had made some and they were fine, but Pam had somehow mis-estimated, because there were more doughnuts than, from the ingredients involved, seemed conceivable. They had made doughnuts until after two in the morning, taking turns frying them, and by that time everything in the house was full of doughnuts and so were the Norths. They were full of doughnuts for several days and after that they were not much interested in doughnuts for a long time, and never again in making them. That, of course, was pre-war; post-war would unquestionably be different. There would, Mr. North thought, eyeing the manuscript, be little room for doughnuts in the post-war world.

"Hmmm!" Pam said. Jerry looked at her and she was looking into the bowl and had stopped turning the egg beater. He deduced that the sound, which had not really so much form even as "hmmm," invited him to conversation.

"Cake?" he said, by way of conversation.

"As far as I can see," Pam North said, "it's whipped cream and always will be. Of course not, Jerry! At ten o'clock at night?"

"Not a cake," Jerry said. He thought. "Pie?" he said, a little hopefully.

"You don't beat a pie," Pam said. "And it would still be ten o'clock at night, wouldn't it?"

"I see what you mean," Jerry said.

"Butter," Pam said. "Only it isn't. And it's *been* half an hour. Or almost."

"Butter?" Jerry said.

Pam said of course butter. What did he think?

"Well," Jerry said. "I didn't think butter. I thought we didn't have any butter. I thought you had spent your red points up through December."

"November," Mrs. North said. "It's very nice of Morris, but sometimes I think it's illegal. Do you suppose it is?"

Jerry said he supposed it was, in a fairly mild way. But it all came out pretty much the same in the end.

"Except," Pam said, "when they end it we'll be ahead, you know. And where will Morris be?"

Morris, Mr. North thought, would be all right.

"Anyway," Pam said, "there wasn't any other way I could think of, and he said it was all right to take them in advance. Of course, it would be different if we had children. It's different for people with children. Particularly babies." Mrs. North resumed grinding the egg beater. "Babies really pay off," she said. "Nothing but milk, or blue points at the worst. Before they abolished them."

"Listen," Jerry said, pulling himself away from the idea that someone had abolished babies. "What about butter? I thought you couldn't use any more butter. I thought it was straight olive oil from here on in."

"Of course we can't use butter," Pam said. "That's why I'm making it."

"You're —" Jerry said and paused — "you're making butter?"

"Why not?" Pam said. "Only apparently I'm not. It's still whipped cream. And they told me it wouldn't be more than half an hour."

"You mean," Jerry said, "that you're sitting there, in a play suit, making butter? *Butter?*"

"Of course," Pam said. "Churning, really. You take some cream — except the cream's so thin now you have to take the top of milk, except the milk's pretty thin too — and beat it until it's butter. If ever, which I doubt. Here, you churn."

She lifted the bowl from her lap and held it toward Jerry, who got up and went over to the sofa and sat down beside her and looked into the bowl. It was full of whipped cream, sure enough. He said so. He said it just looked like whipped cream to him.

"Although come to think of it," he said, "my

mother used to say to look out it didn't turn to butter. That was when I was a boy, of course."

"Well," Pam said. "There still is butter, even if you aren't a boy. And everybody says it will work. Beat, Jerry!"

Jerry beat. He held the egg beater in his left hand and twirled with his right and the beater made a deep, intricate swirl in the soft, yellowish whipped cream.

"You know," Jerry said, after a while, "I never thought we'd be churning here in a New York apartment. Ten floors up, particularly. Did you?"

Pam said it was the war. The war changed a lot of things and the changes had outlasted it. They both looked into the bowl, trying to see the future in it. Then Pam spoke, suddenly.

"Jerry!" she said. "You're spattering!"

"I—" Jerry began, and stopped. He was certainly spattering. Because, as suddenly as Pam had spoken, the whipped cream had come apart. Part of it was thin and spattering and part of it—

"For God's sake!" Jerry said, in a shocked voice. "Butter!"

It was butter. It was sticking to the egg beater. There was not a great deal of it. It was not exactly a solid. But it was beyond doubt butter.

24

The Norths looked at one another with surprise and delight and disbelief.

"Jerry!" Pam said. *"We made butter!"*

"I know," Jerry said. "It's like — like finding gold. Or a good manuscript. It's — it's very strange."

They took the bowl out to the kitchen and scraped the butter off the egg beater and poured off what they supposed was buttermilk — although it didn't taste like buttermilk — and squeezed the water out of the butter as Pam had been told to do. And they were wrapping up almost a quarter of a pound of butter in oiled paper, and still not really believing it, when the telephone rang. Pam was wrapping, and thereupon wrapped more intently, so Jerry was stuck with the telephone.

The voice on the telephone was familiar, and Jerry said, "Yes, Bill?" When she heard him, Pamela put the butter into the icebox quickly and came in and stood in front of Jerry and made faces until he noticed her. Jerry said, "Wait a minute, Bill," and when he looked at her Pam spoke.

"Tell him we made butter," she said. "Tell him he's the first to know."

"Pam says we made butter, Bill," Jerry said. "We did, too. Almost a quarter of a pound."

He listened.

"What did he say?" Pam said.

"He said 'well,' " Jerry told her.

"Was he excited?" Pam wanted to know.

"Were you excited, Bill?" Jerry said into the telephone. Then he spoke to Pam. "He says 'reasonably,' " Jerry told her. "But he says he's got a murder if we don't mind."

"Oh," Pam said. "All right. Tell him we're sorry."

"Pam says we're sorry, Bill," Jerry said into the telephone. "What?"

His voice was suddenly different and, as she heard the change, Pam's own expressive face was shadowed. Because something Bill had said had made murder real to Jerry, and that would make it real to her. She did not want murder to be real again — not ever again.

"Yes," he said. "A woman fiftyish — solidly built — gray hair? With a *p* instead of a *b* as it happens. She's been working for us. At the office. Research."

He listened for almost a minute and there was a queer expression on his face. Then he seemed to break in.

"I can explain that," he said. "She was doing research for us — preliminary research. For a book we're getting out on the subject. Do you want the details?"

He listened again.

26

"Naturally," he said. "She has relatives in the city, I think. But I'll come around. Although from what you say there doesn't seem to be much doubt."

He listened again.

"All right," he said. "The morgue. I'll be along."

He replaced the receiver and looked at Pam a moment, his thoughts far from her. Then he brought them back.

"A woman named Amelia Gipson," he said. "She was working at the office — had been for about a month. Somebody seems to have poisoned her. In the Public Library, of all places. Bill wants me to make a preliminary identification before he gets in touch with her relatives."

"In the Public Library?" Pam said. "At Forty-second Street? The big one?"

Jerry nodded.

"What a strange place," Pam North said. "It's — it's always so quiet there."

"Yes," Jerry said. "She was reading about murders at the time, apparently. For us. For the murder book I told you about. *My Favorite Murder* — working title. Remember?"

Pam said she remembered. With a writer for each crime — a writer who wrote about murder. She remembered.

"Miss Gipson was getting together preliminary data," Jerry said. "We promised them that. It was an odd job for her, come to think of it. She used to be a college professor — or something like it. Anyway, she used to teach in a college. She was a trained researcher. But it was an odd job for her."

It ended oddly enough, Pam thought, and said. It ended very oddly.

"I think I'll go with you," Pam said then. "It's so strange about it's being the Public Library."

Jerry thought she shouldn't, but she did.

The body was under a sheet and they pulled the sheet back from the face. Confidence no longer sat on the face; the features were twisted, curiously. But it was Amelia Gipson and Jerry turned to Lieut. William Weigand of Homicide and nodded.

"What?" Jerry said. "And how?"

Bill Weigand told him what.

"I don't know how," he said. "Suddenly, sitting in the Library, she was very sick. As she would be. Then in about an hour she was dead. In Bellevue. That's all we know, at the moment."

"You don't eat anything in the Library," Pam pointed out. "Do you?"

Bill smiled faintly and shook his head. That was it, he said; that was part of it. Unless you were on the staff, you didn't eat in the Library. You didn't drink.

"So," Jerry pointed out, "she had taken it — had been given it — before she went to the Library."

Bill Weigand shook his head. He said the time didn't fit. He said she had been at the Library for something like two hours — probably more — when she became ill.

"It doesn't wait that long," he said. "We've established that. The dose she seems to have got would have made her violently ill in half an hour or so. Her book slips were time stamped at 7:33. Allow her some time to find the books she wanted in the catalogues, fill out the slips — say a quarter of an hour — and we have her in the Library at fifteen after seven, or thereabouts. Of course, she may have left the Library and come back. If she didn't, she was poisoned in the Library. Presumably while she was sitting at one of the tables in the reading room — the North Reading Room."

"You mean," Pam said, "somebody just came along and said 'Sorry to interrupt your reading, but do you mind drinking some poison?' Because I don't believe it."

"Not that way, obviously," Jerry said. "You're getting jumpy, Pam."

"Not any way like it that I can see," Pam said.

"And I'm not getting jumpy. Do you, Bill?"

Practice helped. Bill did not even have to check back to the clause before the clause.

"It doesn't seem possible," he said. "And it happened. Therefore — a job for us. For Deputy Chief Inspector Artemus O'Malley and his helpers. Mullins. Stein. Me."

"Well," Pam said. "She worked in Jerry's office." It was merely statement; it held implications.

Mullins was in the shadows. Mullins spoke.

"O'Malley won't like it, loot," Mullins said. "He sure as hell won't like it. He likes 'em kept simple."

"But," Pam said, "it isn't simple. Hello, Sergeant Mullins. Is it?"

"Hello, Mrs. North," Mullins said. "No. But the inspector don't want you in none of them. None. He says you *make* 'em complicated. Hard, sort of."

"All right, sergeant," Bill Weigand said, and there was only a thin edge of amusement in his voice. "She was an employee of Mr. North. It was inevitable that we call him. For the moment — until we get in touch with her relatives — we can assume he represents her interests. Right?"

"Say," Mullins said. "That's right, ain't it, loot?"

"Of course it is," Pam said. "Where do we go, Bill? First?"

Bill shrugged. There were a hundred directions. The Library. The office of North Books, Inc. Amelia Gipson's apartment.

"Mullins is going to the Library," he said. "Stein's there, and some of the boys. I'm going to the apartment." He paused and smiled a little. "I should think," he said, "that Jerry has a right to accompany me, Pam."

"So should I," Pam North said. "Shall we start now? It isn't — it isn't very nice in here." She looked around the morgue. "It never is," she said, thoughtfully.

While Bill Weigand picked up a parcel containing Miss Gipson's handbag, and signed a receipt for it, and while they got into the big police car Pam had been silent. Now, as they started toward Washington Square and the Holborn Annex she spoke.

"Why," Pam said, "didn't she kill herself?"

"Miss Gipson?" Jerry said, in a startled voice. "She would no more. . . ." Then he broke off and looked at Bill. "Which is true," he said, after a moment. "She wouldn't think of it — wouldn't have thought of it. But you didn't know that, Bill. How did you know?"

Bill nodded. He said he had been wondering

31

why they didn't ask him that.

"That's the way Inspector O'Malley wanted it," he said. "That's the way he thinks it ought to be. Simple. Suicide. Unfortunately, she wrote us a note."

"What kind of a note?" Pam said. "Non-suicide note?"

Weigand looked at Pam North with approval. He said, "Right."

"She was taking notes," he said. "On the Purdy murder. Writing them out very carefully in a notebook, in ink — very carefully and clearly. And we almost missed her note to us — did miss it the first time. Then Stein thought that while the last thing she had written almost fitted, it didn't really fit. The last thing she wrote was: 'I have been poisoned by —! It didn't finish. Just 'I have been poisoned by —' and a scraggly line running off the page."

"Then how," Pam said, "can even — can the inspector think it was suicide. If he still does."

Bill Weigand said the inspector still wanted to.

"And," he said, "he can make a talking point. You see, she was taking notes on a poison case. The death of a woman named Lorraine Purdy, who was killed, curiously enough, with sodium fluoride. Presumably by her husband, although we were supposed to think by accident. But it

32

wasn't accident — it was Purdy. He ran for it and got himself killed in an airplane accident. O'Malley wants to think that the last thing Miss Gipson wrote was part of her notes on the Purdy case."

He smiled faintly.

"We can't let him," he said. "It almost fits. It doesn't fit. Why was she taking notes on the Purdy case, Jerry?"

Jerry explained that. It was not only the Purdy case. It was a series of cases — ten murder cases, all famous, all American. Her notes were to go to selected writers who were accepted as specialists in crime. "Like Edmund Pearson was," Jerry amplified. Each was to write the story of one of the murders as a chapter in a book. Jerry was to publish the book. It had been his idea. It was not, he added, a new idea. Other publishers had done it; he had done it before himself, several years earlier. There was always a market for crime. As Pearson had proved; as Woollcott had proved; as dozens of lesser writers had proved.

"We did the digging for them," Jerry said. "Miss Gipson did the digging for us. She was a researcher."

When he decided on publishing the book and had needed somebody to do research, Jerry had decided against tying up anybody on his own staff — a rather small staff these days — on a long and detailed job. He had gone to a college placement bureau and Miss Gipson was the result. The rather unexpected result.

"I'd supposed we'd get a girl just out of college," Jerry North said. "Most of them are — the research girls. Miss Gipson was a surprise. She'd been a Latin teacher in a small, very good college for girls in Indiana — Ward College, I think it was. She got tired of it or something and decided on a new field. She was a little surprised when it turned out to be murder research, but she was doing a good job."

"I think," Pam said, "she carried it too far."

They looked at her.

"I only mean," she said, "you don't have to go to the length of getting murdered. It's too — thorough."

The two men looked at each other and after a while Jerry said "oh."